Happy Christmas!

For Amelia and Eliza – my sources of inspiration

Croc-A-Doodle-Doo!
First published 2022
ISBN: 978-1-3999-3884-6

Text Copyright © Sam Payne
Illustration Copyright © Sarah-Leigh Wills

Illustration and Design by: Happydesigner

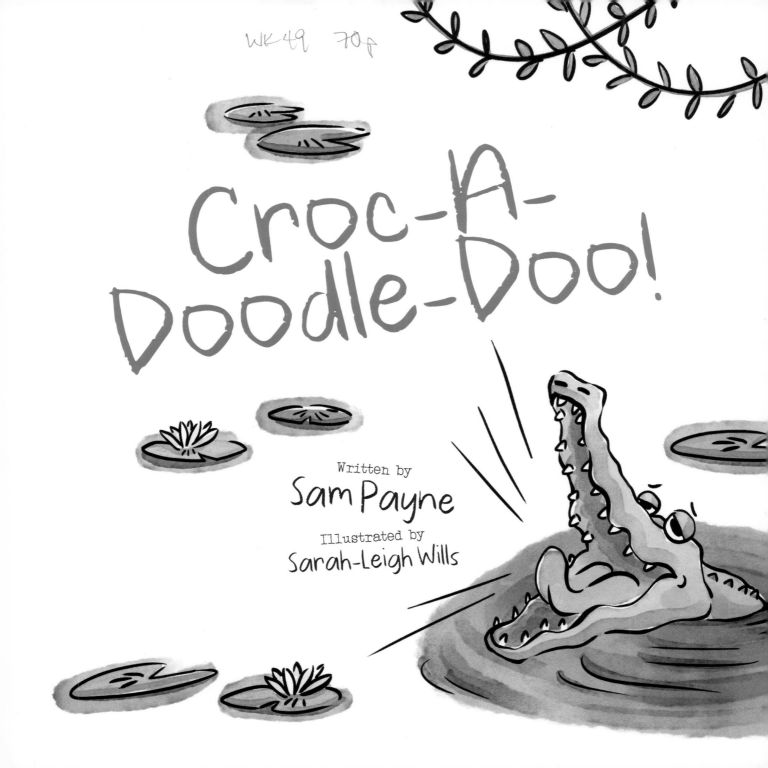

Croc-A-Doodle-Doo!

Written by
Sam Payne

Illustrated by
Sarah-Leigh Wills

Through the murk of the lake
And reflection of sky
Two beady black eyes
Glide silently by

They've spied a plump cockerel
Dance out on a ledge
He's much too close
Too close to the edge

He's glimpsed his reflection
And is having a peek
But danger approaches
Right under his beak

Without warning
And quick as a flash
The cockerel is swallowed
And gone in a splash!

The croc dives back down
So pleased with his plunder
But it soon becomes clear
He's made quite the blunder

For when he opens his jaws
Under his scaly green snout
A 'Cock-a-doodle-doo!'
Comes bellowing out!

His eyes all a panic
And though he tries as he might
'Cock-a-doodle-doo!'
Croc clasps his jaws tight

This noise draws a crowd
Other animals are curious
Another 'Cock-a-doodle-doo!'
And Crocodile is furious!

Ashamed, he dives under
With appearances to keep
No-one will hear him
Down here in the deep

Croc is now stricken
And all of a lather
He hatches a plan
As more fish start to gather

A flick of his tail
And a powerful push
The croc breaks the surface
In a panicky rush

On the riverbank he lands
With an almighty thud
And the force spits out Cockerel
Head first in the mud!

The pair share a moment
As they regather their pride
Hoping nobody noticed
They slope off to hide

But notice they did
What a spectacle to savour
For the silly young bird
Had done them a favour

Now whenever the croc
Approaches his prey
'Cock-a-doodle-doo!'
Gets shouted his way

Regardless of creature
The fierce, or the meek
The croc turns and flees
On hearing them shriek